Caliban's Cave

Poems by Judith Nicholls
Illustrations by Judy Musselle

Collins

Contents

Dream Journey

Open eyes wide,
gaze into the wind.
Stare at sea or land,
leave thoughts behind.
Most of all, *don't talk!*
Soon you will see inside ...

Now, let your mind
take *you* for a walk!

River Song

Water laps, laps
at the river's edge,
watched silently
by grass and tree.

Water flows, flows
beyond the banks,
a tireless traveller
to a distant sea.

Fishing Song

Ragworm, lugworm, mackerel, maggot,
Grey pike lurking, still as steel.
Cast my rod in the deep dark stream
With a nugget of bread for a silver bream.
                    Caught an eel.

Ragworm, lugworm, mackerel, maggot,
Number Ten hook and I'm waiting still.
A carp would be good or a spiny perch,
A golden rudd or a red-finned roach?
                    It's an eel.

Ragworm, lugworm, mackerel, maggot,
Something's biting, wind up the reel!
Is it a pike or a roach or a rudd?
A hunting gudgeon from the river bed?
                    Just – an eel.

Fishy Business

We love to dive through the ocean deep,
below the land where the wild winds blow.
We love to hide behind the weed,
and feel the water's ebb and flow.

We love to wiggle through the waves
where pale fish wander to and fro.
We love to glide beneath the stars
then drift to the sands below.

Storm Tide

The rise of the tide is a white-wave ride
as seas glide in to the shore;
wild surf flies to the watching skies
while winds and waters roar.

The fall of the tide is a lulling ride
with the loud waves' anger gone;
a tired sea slinks sheepishly
from the shore to its ocean home.

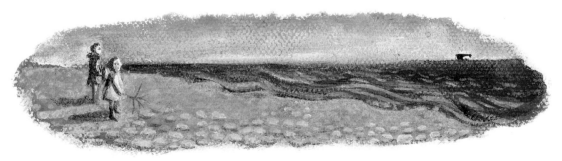

To the Sea!

Who'll be first?
Shoes off,
in a row,
four legs fast,
two legs slow –
Ready now?
off we go!

Tip-toe,
dip-a-toe,
heel and toe –
Yes or no?
Cold as snow!
All at once,
in we go!
One,

     two,

       three,

    SPLASH!

Picnic

There's ...
ham with sand,
and spam with sand,
there's chicken paste
and lamb with sand;
oranges, bananas,
lemonade or tea;
bread with sand
all spread with sand –
at least the sand comes free!
We've crisps with sand
and cake with sand –
it's grand with lunch or tea –
crunch it up,
enjoy it, love,
at least we're by the sea!

10

Eight Things to Do on a Beach

Stretch out on hot sand,
wriggle fingers warmed by sun.

Catch a wave in a bucket;
circle your castle with a hundred shells,
then choose your favourite one.

Smell the sea-salt air,
taste breeze-blown sand in picnic bread;
remember the cry of seagulls
when day is done.

Starfish

Went star-fishing last night.
Dipped my net in the inky lake
To catch a star for my collection.
All I did was shattered the moon.

Sea Dream

I wander the deep-sea forests
where the snake-fish slither;
where the dark dunes drift
like rolling mist
and the white whales murmur.

I wake to coral blossom
and sleep in a star-clad cave;
my bed is a glade
of ribboned jade,
my sky a wave.

I dance by the spiny urchin
and ride the giant clam;
I feel as I sail
the dolphin's tail
the sad whale song.

Lord Neptune

Build me a castle,
the young boy cried,
as he tapped his father's knee.
But make it tall
and make it wide,
with a king's throne just for me.

An echo drifted on the wind,
sang deep and wild and free:
Oh you can be king of the castle,
but I am lord of the sea.

Give me your spade,
the father cried;
let's see what we can do!
We'll make it wide
so it holds the tide,
with a fine throne just for you.

He dug deep down
in the firm damp sand,
for the tide was falling fast.
The moat was deep,
the ramparts high,
and the turrets tall and vast.

Now I am king,
the young boy cried,
and this is my golden throne!
I rule the sands,
I rule the seas;
I'm lord of all lands, alone!

15

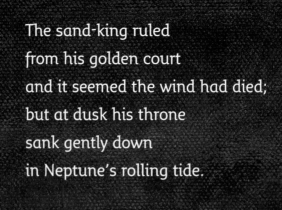

The sand-king ruled
from his golden court
and it seemed the wind had died;
but at dusk his throne
sank gently down
in Neptune's rolling tide.

And an echo rose upon the wind,
sang deep and wild and free:
Oh you may be king of the castle,
but I am lord of the sea.

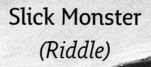

Slick Monster
(Riddle)

Velvet black wave
gently laps the shore;
small white seagull
flies no more.

Shiny black monster
slowly creeps to land;
small pink crab
buried in the sand.

Answer: oil slick

17

Goodwin Sands

I have seen the pale gulls circle
against a restless sky;
I have heard the dark winds crying
as dusk-drawn clouds wheel by.

But the waiting waves still whisper
of shadowy ocean lands,
of twisting tides and of secrets
that lie beneath the Sands.

18

I have seen the wild weeds' tangle
and smelt the salted squall;
I have seen the moon rise from the seas,
and felt the long night's fall.

But whose are the voices that echo
from the shifting ocean lands,
that tell of secrets buried
beneath the drifting Sands?

For many sail the Goodwins
and some return to shore;
but others ride in the falling tide
and those are seen no more.

And voices rise from the waters
beneath a restless sky:
in the dying light of coming night
the long-lost sailors sigh;
from the watery lands of Goodwin Sands
I hear the sailors cry.

Dolphin Dance

We are darters and divers
from secret sea-caves.
We're dippers and gliders,
we dance through the waves.

We spiral and curl,
we weave as we fly,
stitch shimmering arches
from ocean to sky.

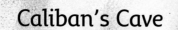

Caliban's Cave

The sand is damp
and cold as stone
when the tide creeps back
from Caliban's Cave.

The rocks are black
as you creep alone
on the dark, damp sand
of Caliban's Cave.

The seagulls sing
and the sea-shells moan
as they slide in the tide
through Caliban's Cave.

The pebbles ring
like the crack of a bone
as you tip-toe deep
into Caliban's Cave.

23

The music dies
when the waves have gone
and you stand alone
in Caliban's Cave ...

You stand in the heart
of Caliban's Cave ...

Earthset

Night spreads like purple heather
over wasteland sky
and marbled earth rolls gently into sleep.

Haiku of the Four Winds

The wind of the north
hurls itself over lonely oceans,
breathing ice into earth's lungs.

The wind from the east
is a sharp-toothed beast, wilfully
biting into day.

26

The wind from the south
slithers through summer grasses,
made lazy by sun.

The wind from the west
is a wind of rest, drifting,
whispering from the sunset ...

What Is the Wind?

Wind is a thief,
a stealer of leaves.
He scatters them far
from their golden trees.

Wind is a sneak,
a stirrer of seas.
He's a hurler of hats
to the autumn breeze.

Wind is a thief,
with no wish to please.
Wind is a snatcher,
a robber, a tease!

Forest End

Since they left the house
the trees moved in;
the oak and ash made a home.
Where the chimney stood
is a jagged pine,
and the roof has almost gone.

Since they left the house
the birds moved in;
you can hear the thrush's song.
The house awakes
to the squawk of rooks,
and sleeps when the owl has flown.

Since they left the house
the winds moved in;
the windows wail and groan.
A few stairs creak
to a clouded sky,
then the house is left, alone.

31

What on Earth?

What on earth are we doing?
Once wood-pigeons flew,
and young badgers tunnelled
where oak and ash grew ...

Now the forest's a runway,
and all that flies through
is a whining grey plane
where the pigeons once flew.

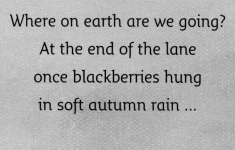

Where on earth are we going?
At the end of the lane
once blackberries hung
in soft autumn rain ...

Now the lane is a car park,
and never again
will fruit fill our baskets
down in the lane.

33

Why on earth are we crying?
Once morning dew shone
on hawthorn and primrose,
caught in the sun ...

Now the forest is carpeted
only with stone.
No primrose, no hawthorn;
the forest has gone.

Would You ...?

How would you like to see
earth's face shaved clean
of grass and tree?
Not me!

How would you like to hear
the sound of thrush
and robin disappear?
No fear!

How would you like to try
to live upon an earth
where forests die?
Not I!

Progress Man!

Hurry now! *cried Progress*,
just see what I can do!
Watch my chain saw, feel my axe;
my ways are great for you,

'cos I'm a swinging, singing,
racing, chasing, do-it-how-I-can,
I'm the swinging, singing,
racing, chasing Progress Man!

See me chop your forests down,
we need a motorway!
You have some roads already ...?
Well, not enough, I say,

and I'm a swinging, singing,
racing, chasing, do-it-how-I-can,
I'm the swinging, singing,
racing, chasing Progress Man!

What's a little drop of oil
spilt over golden sand?
It's just a tiny price to pay,
the world has so much land,

and I'm a swinging, singing,
racing, chasing, do-it-how-I-can,
I'm the swinging, singing,
racing, chasing Progress Man!

Firelight

Last night
as flames curled round my coal
I thought I saw
a million years ago
a forest fall.

Give Me Your Name ...

Give me your name
and I will
fire it out of a cannon,
I'll stretch it from mountain to mountain
like a giant elastic band,
I'll feed it to the falcons
to drop it on the sand,
I'll tie it to a kite
and fly it through the snow,
I'll plant it in a valley
and wait and watch it grow.

I'll pour it into a searchlight
and beam it through the night,
I'll hang it beneath the moon
like a moth in graceful flight.
I'll give it to the mermaids
and weave it through the waves,
I'll bury it on the ocean bed
in the deepest, darkest cave.
I'll throw it into a river,
let it flow down to the sea,
I'll hide it by the willows

... if you give your name to me!

*Written with Parsons Down Poets in Schools Group
Feb 1996*

Something to Do in a Traffic Jam

Dream of
a world where bat
and tiger wander free
and turtles set their courses by
the stars.

Journey

I spread my wings
with the wild geese,
I wander the hills
and the skies.
I rise over field and river,
behind the wild goose cries.
One day I'll return
to surprise you ...

stronger, taller,
and wise.

What Is One?

One is the sun,
a rhino's horn;
a drop of dew,
a lizard's tongue.

One is the world,
a lonely whale;
an elephant's trunk,
a monkey's tail.

One is an acorn,
one is a moon;
one is a forest,
felled too soon.

Dreamtime

A sleep-glazed sun slips through the streets
and rolls down hills and streams;
but before it leaves at close of day
it seems to pause at earth's edge to say,
Cry goodbye to your daytime world;
sing hello to your dreams.

Soon darkness cloaks the streets and parks
and only a half-moon gleams.
It hovers there like the ghost of a kite
which seems to sigh through the star-filled night,
Cry goodbye to your daytime world;
sing hello to your dreams.

Save the planet

We are darters and divers
from secret sea-caves.

Since they left the house
the trees moved in;
the oak and ash made a home.

At the end of the lane
once blackberries hung

I spread my wings
with the wild geese,

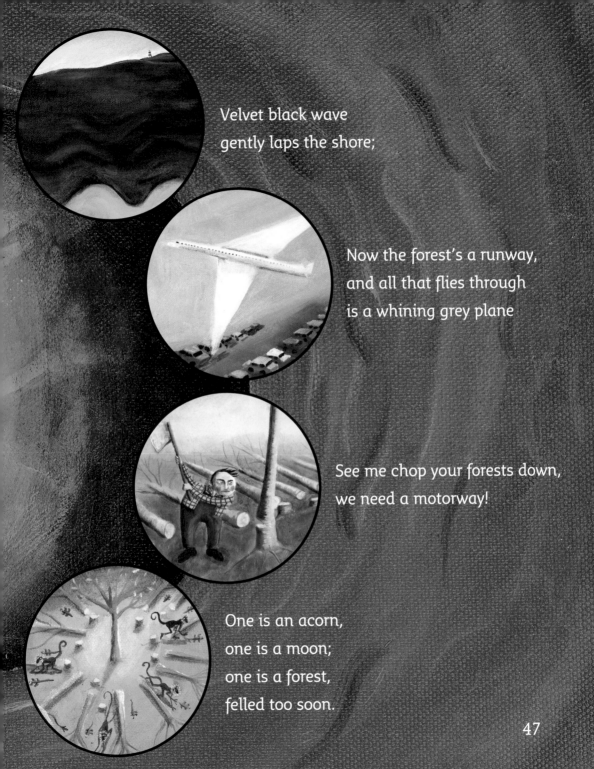

Velvet black wave
gently laps the shore;

Now the forest's a runway,
and all that flies through
is a whining grey plane

See me chop your forests down,
we need a motorway!

One is an acorn,
one is a moon;
one is a forest,
felled too soon.

Ideas for guided reading

Learning objectives: explain how writers use figurative and expressive language; show imagination through the language used; comment constructively on performance

Curriculum links: Science: Habitats; Citizenship: Respect for property

Interest words: tireless, ragworm, lugworm, mackerel, nugget, gudgeon, sheepishly, urchin, squall, wasteland, marbled, hawthorn, falcon

Resources: pens, poster paper

Getting started

This book can be read over two or more guided reading sessions.

- Invite one of the children to read the blurb aloud to others. Explain that the blurb is a few lines from the poem "Caliban's Cave".

- Ask children if anyone has heard the name Caliban. Explain that it is the name of a magician from another story (Shakespeare's *The Tempest*).

- Ask children what the description of *Caliban's Cave* and the picture on the front cover suggest, e.g. secrets, mystery.

- Ask children to look through the contents page and to choose a poem they would like to read.

Reading and responding

- Ask children to read the poem they have chosen. Ask them to be prepared to discuss the reason they chose the poem and what they thought of it.

- Working in pairs, ask children to choose other poems to read and to identify recurring themes in the poems, e.g. sea, earth, pollution.

- Ask children to read their selected poems aloud to the group using strategies such as multiple voices, taking turns to read alternate lines and using a different voice for direct speech.